JE
MAY

Mayer, Mercer
Just a daydream

# JUST A DAYDREAM

## BY
## MERCER MAYER

To Daniel Hall

**A GOLDEN BOOK • NEW YORK**

**Western Publishing Company, Inc., Racine, Wisconsin 53404**

There is a bully in my neighborhood.
Sometimes when we play ball, he takes it.
Then we can't play.

If I have a bag of candy,
he makes me give it to him.

Sometimes he pushes me just for fun.
Then I cry.

If I were Super Critter, then that bully would never bother me.

I'd wear a mask and have a long cape.

I would fly high in the sky.
I'd fly faster than a jet plane.

I would be strong, too. I would be able to lift my dad's car. My dad would be so amazed.

If I saw that bully, I'd pick him up and
carry him to the top of the tallest tree.
I would leave him there until he said
"I'm sorry" fifty million times.

I would make him play with all of the little kids and be their friend.

I would rescue critters from fires and earthquakes.

I would help the police catch robbers and bad guys. I would be able to see through walls, so they couldn't hide from me.

If aliens from a flying saucer
came down to invade Earth,
I would chase them away.

If a dinosaur appeared and started wrecking things and scaring everybody...

I would carry him off to a deserted island so he couldn't hurt anyone.

I would teach him to be nice and to do tricks. He would be my pet.

I would build a big castle on the highest mountain. It would be full of my special Super Critter stuff.

It might be lonely, so I would bring my mom and dad and even my little sister to live with me.

It would be so cool if I were Super Critter.
But I guess I'm not.

"Someone's here to see you, Little Critter," Mom said. It was the bully.

"Here, I wanted to give you back your candy," he said.

"Why are you doing that?" I asked.

"Because a critter with a mask and a cape made me promise to be nice, or he was going to put me on the top of the tallest tree forever.

"Do you want to play ball?"